Mickey Saves Santa

By Sheila Sweeny Higginson
Based on the episode written by Leslie Valdes
Illustrated by the Disney Storybook Artists

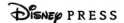 **DISNEP PRESS**

New York

APR 2010

Disney PRESS

First Paperback Edition
Library of Congress Cataloging-in-Publication Data on file
ISBN 978-1-4231-1846-6 $14.96

Manufactured in the USA
For more Disney Press fun, visit www.disneybooks.com

'Twas the day before Christmas,
When in the Clubhouse . . .

The friends had all gathered
Around Mickey Mouse.

They gave Mickey lists that were written with care,
And each hoped that Santa Claus soon would be there.

Donald sat by a fire that burned gold and red,
While visions of fire trucks danced in his head.

When up on the roof there arose such a clatter,
The friends ran to the door to see what was the matter.

When, what to their wondering eyes should appear,
But Mrs. Claus riding a flying reindeer.

She greeted the friends and then let them all know
That without Mickey's help, Santa might never show.

"Santa's in trouble. Please, go right away,
To Mistletoe Mount, where he's stuck in his sleigh!"

Mickey explained there was no need to worry.
"My good friends and I will get there in a hurry!"

He grabbed Mouseketools and took Donald along.
Then they jumped in the Toon Plane and shouted, "So long!"

They zoomed through the sky on that cold winter day,
And Toodles was there to help guide their way.

Then, suddenly, clouds began blocking the sky.
"We need help right now!" Donald started to cry.

Toodles came to the rescue without a delay,
With a spotlight to shine through the sky dark and gray.

And just when the North Pole appeared very near,
They ran out of gas; Donald shivered with fear.

"Oh, no!" shouted Mickey. "Please help us get down!
Count backward from ten to get us to the ground!"

The friends looked around and could see Mistletoe,
But they didn't know how to get through all the snow.

Then Toodles showed up with a tool they could wear.
Each friend got a package of skis in a pair.

"There's Santa! Oh, gosh! Are his reindeer all here?"
Mickey counted to eight and then gave a big cheer.

But Santa showed Mickey his sled that had stopped—
With a harness so broken it just sadly flopped.

Then a mystery tool helped to save Christmas Day:
The friends helped tie ribbons to fix Santa's sleigh!

"Merry Christmas to all,
And to all a good night!"